MY PLACE

Nadia Wheatley & Donna Rawlins

WALKER BOOKS
AND SUBSIDIARIES

LONDON • BOSTON • SYDNEY • AUCKLAND

My name's Laura and this is my place. I turned ten last week. Our house is the one with the flag on the window. Tony says it shows we're on Aboriginal land, but I think it means the colour of the earth, back home. Mum and Dad live here too, and Terry and Lorraine, and Auntie Bev, and Tony and Diane and their baby Dean. He's my nephew and he's so cute! We come from Bourke, but Dad thought there'd be more jobs in the city.

This is me and Gully. I have to keep her on a lead because she chases cars. She comes from Bourke too. I guess she thinks they're sheep.

This is a map of my place. At the top of the street there is the biggest fig tree you've ever seen! Whenever I climb up and sit in it, I always feel really good. There's a canal down the bottom of the street, and Mum says it must have been a creek once. It's too dirty to swim in, but Tony made me a tin canoe and now some of the other kids are making them too. If you tip over and go in, the water tastes yucky and your parents go wild.

Church and graveyard
Cop shop
Cakes Pies
old furniture
Lebanese takeaway
Post Office
newspapers
Service station

My new School
THE BICENTENNIAL HOTEL
Old Junk yard
St Vdep Op shop
Vietnamese cafe
Greek deli
Bread shop
Park view restaurant
Thai restaurant
empty
Hamburgers
Dry cleaner
RAILWAY PUB
STATION

chimneys

THEY'RE BULLDOZING IN THE OLD TIP

FLATS

BIG TREE WITH LAWN UNDER IT
McDONALDS
CAR PARK
LANE

FLATS

Vietnamese Grocery
FLATS
FLATS
TRAFFIC LIGHTS

houses

All this colour is houses

MY PLACE → HOME

My friend Bianca lives here →

My friend Soriya lives here
LANE

My friend Tamara lives here
TRUCK YARD

My friend Fatima lives here

houses

LANE
warehouse

This road is really busy. Gully isn't allowed up here.
There's a bridge over that way along the canal but I couldn't fit it in. Planes fly that way.

BRICK PITS PARK
It's only just opened this year

TRACK (THERE'S A FENCE WITH LOTS OF GOOD HOLES)
CANAL

OLD FACTORIES AND STUFF
OLD WOODEN BUILDINGS

For my birthday, Mum said we could have a picnic. We went and sat down under the tree, and it felt just like home.

FEED THE WORLD

This is my place. I'm Mike. I'm nearly seven. I live with Mum and Dad and Yaya and Auntie Sofia. Yaya's my grandmother, but I call her that because she's Greek. I don't speak very much Greek, but I kind of always understand what she's saying.

We have Easter lunch in the backyard under the grapevine. There's roast lamb and salad, and of course I get chocolate eggs, but we have red real eggs too, and we have a competition about cracking them. I'm the best at it.

This is me and Whiskers. He sneaks in and sleeps on my bed.

STATION

houses

houses
School

Old Junk yard

Hamburgers

My other Nanna lives here ✗

Old Church
graves ↓

Sandwiches
Lebanese take away
empty
P.O
paper shop
Service station

Old Skating rink (Closed

Pub
milk Bar
Deli
Bread and Cakes

old fridges and stoves

Pub

The Tip
Trucks come and dump old Cars and Stuff here

↑ The Lollypop man guards the crossing

Flats

Flats

office
BIG TREE
CAR YARD
LANE

BIG

Flats

We used to shop here but it's closed because people go to the supermarket

These are meant to be chimneys

They're bulldozing all around the old chimneys. It's like a huge puddle when it rains

more houses

The planes fly over here

houses

houses

MY PLACE
my best friend Ben's house →

LANE

TRUCK YARD
LANE
Warehouses

Big bridge
← TRACK

↙ ← OVERSEAS
old factory

CANAL
old factory

old factory

Falling down warehouses

TRACK ↓

This is a map of my place. When you're up the top of the big tree and a jet goes over, you feel as if you're going to fall out. Mum wants to move because of all the noise, but I like aeroplanes and trucks and stuff. Auntie Sofia and I often go down to the canal. She says that if you went down it, and into the river, then into the bay, you'd be on your way to Overseas!

My name's Sofia and this is my place. I'm ten. Baba's just painted our house blue.
He comes from Greece, and he says lots of houses on his island were this colour.
I think it's really pretty. I live with Mama and Baba and Maroula and Paul McCartney.
I've got a big brother called Michaelis, but he's a soldier in Vietnam. Mama lights
candles to pray that he comes home soon and isn't hurt.

This is me and Paul McCartney. Maroula reckons John Lennon's best, but I like Paul.

Before Michaelis went away, we had a goodbye party and he invited a girlfriend! She looked a bit left out because all of us were speaking Greek mostly. Michaelis looked weird in his new haircut. He didn't want to go, but he said the law said he had to. I wish that war would stop.

All the yellow means houses.

Michaelis' girlfriend lives over here somewhere ⊗

Old graves- we play here

My (YUK) School

Police

PIE SHOP

BUTCHER

EMPTY

POST OFFICE

NEWS AGENT

Petrol Station

Junk yard

Maroula works here

PUB

ICE SKATING

MILK BAR

Deli

Baker

Greek cafe where Baba goes

FURNITURE SHOP

EMPTY

SECOND HAND SHOP

EMPTY

Pub

STATION

You should see the house over here. It's got shells all over the outside and a big butterfly on the gate. Mareka and I wish we lived there!!

More old brickpits. Mareka and I have adventures in them.

A kid from school was run over on the main road. There aren't any crossings or lights.

Flats

Flats

office

BIG TREE

They make garden statues and fountains here

Shed   Shed

Baba rents the shed for his truck

Mareka lives here (She's my best friend)

MY PLACE

LOTS OF PLANES GO OVER

Shop where we go

New flats

New flats

Truck yard

Warehouses

Last year the brickpits closed. My dad says they can't use the land for anything because it could all cave in. (They've left the chimneys there.)

track and fence

Bridge

CANAL

Closed down   factories   warehouses   warehouses

This is a map of my place. Maroula works at the milk bar. I put messages in bottles and send them down the canal. And sometimes, when I want to think about things, I go up the big tree in the statue yard. There are more people in the street now because of the flats, but they don't seem to have any kids.

1958

This is my place. My name's Michaelis but at school I say it's Mick. I'm eleven. I was born on Kalymnos but my parents moved here because there wasn't enough work on our island. Baba used to be a sponge diver but now he drives a taxi. Mama sews shirts at home, so she doesn't learn to speak English much. I've already got a sister called Maroula, and now I've got a new one called Sofia. You'd think at least one of them could have been a boy.

After Sofia got christened, we had a party. Baba and I had to make a fence so no one would tread on the new grape vine. Sometimes I think there are more Greek people around here than there are on Kalymnos.

This is a map of my place. Pop and Mrs Malcolm next door have got a television, and sometimes they let me go in and watch it! Up near the depot there's a big tree, and I play Tarzan. That and Zorro are my favourite shows. Sometimes at the end of the day our family goes for a little walk beside the canal, like we used to do around the harbour back on Kalymnos. It's pretty dirty, and there aren't any cafes or anything, but Mama says if you shut your eyes you can pretend it's the Aegean.

That stupid girl that kissed me lives over here x
houses

Church but not ours

old grave.

I go to school here

Police
Butcher
fruit shop
P.O
Paper shop
The new service station

PIES

More old brickpits

It's closing soon

You can buy Greek bread here

Taxi rank where Baba often works from x

STATION

BIG Pub
PICTURE THEATRE
MILK BAR
Deli
Baker
Pub Closed
Railway Pub

MAIN ROAD - LOTS OF TRUCKS AND MOTOR BIKES!!

houses

The old brickpits here are closed. Mama says they're dangerous but we play in them

My friends and I ride our bikes along the track.

my mate Christos lives here

Flats

Flats

BIG TREE

TRUCK DEPOT
TRUCKS PARK HERE

OFFICE

DELI

My friend Nick's dad has this deli.

They're knocking down the old soft drink factory

HOUSES

BRICKPITS
x   x
They still use these ones, but not much

X's mean chimneys

HOUSES

HOUSES

Lane
HOUSES
old shed

My friend Wayne lives here →

MY PLACE

Lane

Pop and Mrs malcolm's place

HOUSES

My friend Manolis lives here

warehouses

There's a fence along the canal but it has good holes

track

Bridge →

Shirt factory that Mama works for

CANAL

WE GO FOR WALKS ALONG HERE

These two factories are closed down

Bed spring factory

warehouse

warehouse

warehouse

warehouse

warehouse

warehouse →

This is me and my silkworms. They don't have names. I feed them on mulberry leaves. Their silk is soft and golden.

1948

My name's Jen and this is my place. I'm eight and a half. I live with Mum and Grandpa and Auntie Bridie, and now there's my new dad. My real dad's dead. He went to the war before I was born, so I never even saw him. But Mum says I've got his hair.

When Mum married my new dad, we had a party. Uncle Paddy and Uncle Col came, and Miss Miller from next door and the Malcolms from the other side. Miss Miller's going to be ninety next year! My new dad's got a car. It's green.

There's an old building with lizards carved on the front here.

we play in the old graves

My school

more houses and stuff

Dad gets petrol ↓ Garage

Mum and Auntie Bridie took me to the pictures, but it was all kissing–yuk

Grandpa sometimes goes here The Brickies

COPS

Cake and pie shop

Butcher

grocer

Post office

fruit shop

Empty

paper shop

Pub mum works here

PICTURE THEATRE

MILK BAR

Grocer

Baker

A boy from school got knocked ✗ over here

Big tree

The shop

BRICKPITS

Old Brickpits (They don't use them any more)

Dad says they might put a tip here.

houses

FLATS (MOSTLY EMPTY)

THE HAUNTED HOUSE USED TO BE HERE

DIRT AND STONES

lane

EMPTY

EMPTY

The soft drink factory is still closed

Grandpa used to work here. He says it used to be really busy.

My new dad works at the airport. It's over this way

houses

houses

houses

houses

houses

SHED

MY PLACE

Miss Miller lives here all by herself

Jan lives here she's my best friend

Margie lives here (she's my friend too)

CHIMNEYS

I take Soxie for walks along the track

My second best friend Janey lives here

houses

Pop and mrs malcolm live here

lane

hole in fence

EMPTY

← new fence →

hole in fence

CANAL I saw a boy swimming in here. I'd be in BIG trouble if I did!

It's all factories across this side

This is a map of my place. Mum says when she was a kid there used to be heaps more shops. They're knocking the Haunted House down, but Miss Miller yelled at them and made them promise not to touch the big tree. She told them I've got a swing in it. At the bottom of the street there's a canal. The council's built a fence, but it always seems to get holes in it. Sometimes I fish down there, but I never catch anything.

This is me and Soxie. Dad says we might move out to the western suburbs soon, and get a house with a big yard all around it. But I think Soxie would hate it. He likes how it smells here.

1938

This is my place. I'm Col. I'm almost eleven. In my house there's Pa and Declan and Bridie and Kath and Jack. My ma got pneumonia when I was little, and Paddy's up country somewhere, looking for work. Miss Miller next door is kind of like family too. When Kath and Jack got married, she gave them her piano!

The night the Thomsons got evicted, it was like a party in the street. The bailiffs had stuck all their things out on the footpath and boarded up the house, so Mrs Thomson knocked down the fence and built a big fire. Everyone brought a pot of stew or some spuds or something, and when we'd finished eating, Pa got out his fiddle. It didn't seem awful then, but the next day they went away to the unemployed camp, and we never ever see them any more.

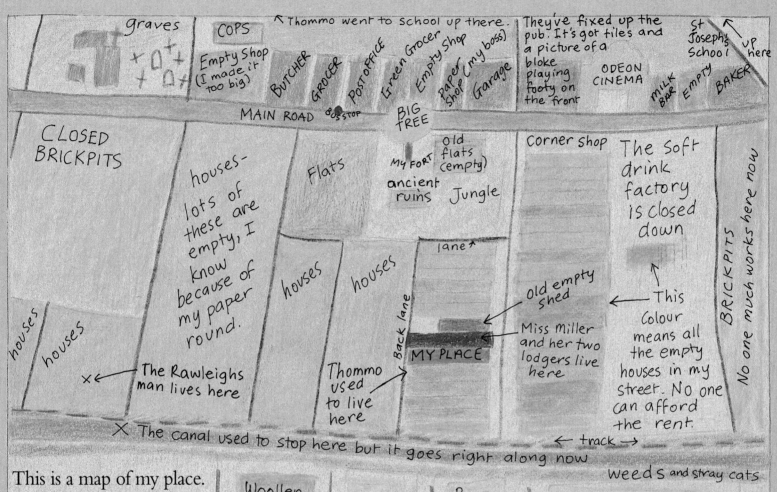

graves

COPS

↑ Thommo went to school up there.

Empty Shop (I made it too big)

BUTCHER

GROCER

POST OFFICE

Green Grocer

Empty Shop

Paper Shop (my boss)

Garage

They've fixed up the pub. It's got tiles and a picture of a bloke playing footy on the front

ODEON CINEMA

St Joseph's School ↑ up here

MILK BAR

EMPTY

BAKER

MAIN ROAD   BUS STOP

BIG TREE

CLOSED BRICKPITS

houses- lots of these are empty, I know because of my paper round.

Flats

MY FORT
ancient ruins

old flats (empty)
Jungle

Corner shop

The Soft drink factory is closed down

houses

houses

lane ↑

old empty shed

← This Colour means all the empty houses in my street. No one can afford the rent.

BRICKPITS

No one much works here now

houses

houses

X ← The Rawleighs man lives here

Thommo used to live here

Back lane

MY PLACE

Miss miller and her two lodgers live here

X The canal used to stop here but it goes right along now

← track →

weeds and stray cats

This is a map of my place. Pa and Declan got put on relief work to turn the creek into a canal, but it's finished and they're back on the dole again. When my mate Thommo still lived here, we nicked some wood from the old house and built a fort in the big tree. And we used to swim in the canal, when our parents weren't around. But now there's no one to muck about with.

Woollen factory. Bridie works here.

FACTORY I don't know what it is but stuff gets on your washing on windy days

BOOT FACTORY (Almost no one works here)

FACTORY YARDS There's two big dogs in here to keep people out.

This is me and Bessie. She's laid her eggs in my billycart, and I can't use it for my paper run. I hope they hurry up and hatch.

1928

My name's Bridie and this is my place. I'm seven. I was born in Dublin, but Pa and Mumma left because there wasn't much work there. Now Pa reckons jobs are getting hard to find here too. The rest of my family is Paddy and Declan and Kathleen and now Colum. Mumma says he was a surprise. Pa and Paddy and Declan all work at the brickworks. Dec had to put his age up because he's only thirteen.

I don't have a pet, but Kath and I look after Col in the afternoon because Mumma cleans at the flats. We put him in the pram and bounce him along the creek track till he goes to sleep. I wish the creek was clean enough to swim in.

This is a map of my place. Last year they put in the poles, so now our lights are electric! It's really exciting living here because the aerodrome's just nearby, and sometimes aeroplanes fly over. I climb up the big tree and wave to the pilots. Mumma says we're lucky here because we've got good neighbours. Miss Miller lets Kath and me play her piano, and if we catch Henry's bus he won't let us pay. The Thomsons on the other side have got a wireless! Lorna Thomson's my best friend.

We had a party last Saint Patrick's Day. He's the Saint of Ireland, and we all wear green for him and sing and dance. Pa got a bit sad because he was missing home, so Mumma invited the Next Doors in to cheer him up.

This is my place. Mum calls me Bertie, but Eddie and all the blokes at the hospital call me Champ. I'm nine. My brother Eddie's only got one leg, but he's still great at cricket. He and the blokes sometimes let me play with them down by the creek. I live with Mum and Eddie and my sister Ev, and we let the front room to Miss Walkley, from church. Dad died at Gallipoli. Miss Walkley says that's something to be proud of, but I reckon it stinks. He was a great spin bowler.

This is me and Gert. We got her to help the War Effort.

This is a map of my place. Mum works in the kitchen at the hospital, and when Ev comes home from the factory she puts on her VAD dress and goes over there too. I've got a treehouse in the big tree. Mum says we might have to move to the country because we can't afford to live here now, but I don't want to.

LOTS OF TRAINS

HOUSES

This place used to make headstones

OUR CHURCH

Miss Walkley plays the organ.

SCHOOL

POLICE

(I think this one is the post office)

P.O

THE BRICKPITS HERE ARE CLOSED NOW

Mr Miller's shop and petrol pumps

CENTENNIAL HOTEL

Shops

BRICKMAKERS ARMS HOTEL

These dots mean electric light poles

LOTS OF TRAFFIC

BRICKPITS

BIG TREE

SQUISHY FIGS

HOSPITAL

CHAIRS AND STUFF FOR THE SOLDIERS

OLD SHEDS

Shops

CORDIAL FACTORY

RAILWAY VIEW HOTEL

BRICKPITS

HOUSES

HOUSES

HOUSES

LANE

Eddie's best mate, Sid, (from the army) lives here

HOUSES

LANE

HOUSES

WE PLAY CRICKET HERE

We had our party here when the war ended

Old shed

Miller's house

MY PLACE

BRICKPITS WITH THE BIGGEST CHIMNEYS

The girl who lives on top of this shop has got a rabbit in a box. Eddie reckons it's safer in the box. He reckons if she lets it out it might end up someone's dinner!

HOUSES

CANAL

ICE WORKS

FACTORY BRIDGE

HOUSES

TRACK

FACTORY

WOOLLEN FACTORY

WOOLLEN FACTORY

IRON FOUNDRY

BOOT FACTORY WHERE EV MAKES SOLDIERS' BOOTS

I GRAZE GERT ON THE WEEDS BESIDE THE TRACK

On the day the war ended, people danced in the street and blokes hugged each other on the lawn. But Mum started crying. Then Miss Miller cried, then Mr Miller even cried, because their Tom and Fred won't be coming home either. So I did some stilt-walking on Eddie's crutches and made them stop.

1908

My name's Evelyn and this is my place. I'm ten. We moved here because it's close to the city for Father to get to the bank. Mother teaches music at the college, but of course Eddie and I go to the ordinary school. On the way home, we always wait near the petrol pump on Müllers' corner in case a motor car stops. Father says the main road will be tar soon, and there'll be even more traffic. Of course, Eddie pesters Father about when we will get a motor car, but you'd have to be as rich as anything for that.

This is me and Old Ned. He used to pull a horse bus but Mr Müller put him out to pasture when the trams went electric. He says poor Ned just couldn't keep up.

Last Cracker Night all our street had a bonfire down near the creek.
We got crackers from the Chinese shop. Mr Müller said it reminded
him of old times.

This is a map of my place. On weekends I play caves under the big tree.
Mr Müller says, when he was a boy, a dragon lived across the creek.
When I was little I used to believe him.

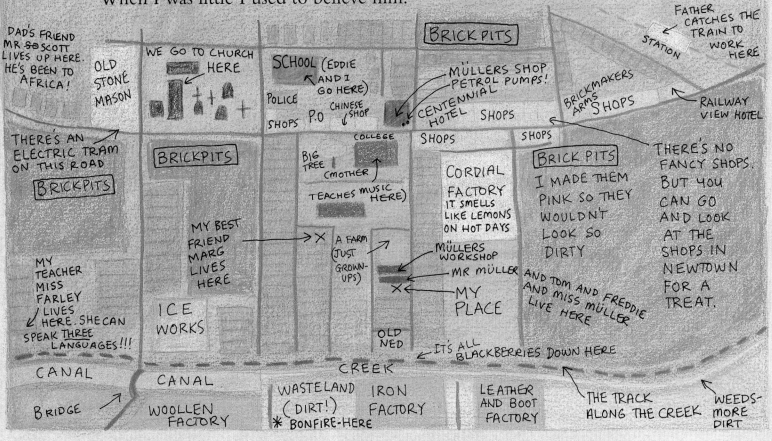

FATHER CATCHES THE TRAIN TO WORK HERE

STATION

DAD'S FRIEND MR SO SCOTT LIVES UP HERE. HE'S BEEN TO AFRICA!

OLD STONE MASON

WE GO TO CHURCH HERE

SCHOOL (EDDIE AND I GO HERE)

BRICK PITS

MÜLLERS SHOP PETROL PUMPS! CENTENNIAL HOTEL

Police

Shops

P.O

CHINESE SHOP

SHOPS

BRICKMAKERS ARMS SHOPS

RAILWAY VIEW HOTEL

THERE'S AN ELECTRIC TRAM ON THIS ROAD

BRICKPITS

BRICKPITS

BIG TREE

COLLEGE

(MOTHER

TEACHES MUSIC HERE)

SHOPS

SHOPS

BRICK PITS

THERE'S NO FANCY SHOPS. BUT YOU CAN GO AND LOOK AT THE SHOPS IN NEWTOWN FOR A TREAT.

MY BEST FRIEND MARG LIVES HERE

X

A FARM (JUST GROWN-UPS)

CORDIAL FACTORY IT SMELLS LIKE LEMONS ON HOT DAYS

MÜLLERS WORKSHOP

MR MÜLLER

I MADE THEM PINK SO THEY WOULDN'T LOOK SO DIRTY

MY TEACHER MISS FARLEY LIVES HERE. SHE CAN SPEAK THREE LANGUAGES!!!

ICE WORKS

X

MY PLACE

AND TOM AND FREDDIE AND MISS MÜLLER LIVE HERE

OLD NED

IT'S ALL BLACKBERRIES DOWN HERE

CANAL

CANAL

CREEK

THE TRACK ALONG THE CREEK

WEEDS-MORE DIRT

BRIDGE

WOOLLEN FACTORY

WASTELAND (DIRT!)
* BONFIRE-HERE

IRON FACTORY

LEATHER AND BOOT FACTORY

1898

This is my place. My name's Rowley. I'm eight. My mum and me, we rent the upstairs front room. Auntie Adie's got the middle room and Miss Singer's got the back. Mum works at the laundry with Auntie Adie. She's not really my auntie, but I call her that. Downstairs, there's Mr Merry. He does photographs, but on weekends he has an icecream cart, and he lets me and Tommy Müller help him. Tom lives next door. His auntie's got a bicycle!

This is a map of my place. The big tree belongs to the posh school, but I climb it anyway. A bit down the creek, it turns into a canal, and there are barges. Before my dad went away, he helped build it. Mum says he just couldn't find any more work, and one day he might come back.

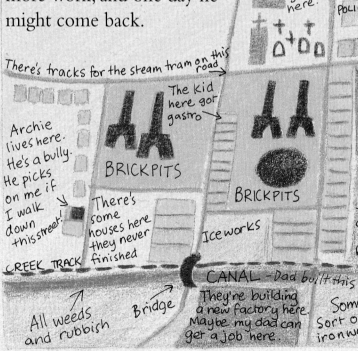

There's tracks for the steam tram on this road

Archie reckons there's ghosts here.

SCHOOL

POLICE

Chinese shop MÜLLERS

P.O.

MORE BRICKPITS

You catch mr Müller's horse bus here

Centennial Hotel. Tommy and me get mr merry's beer here.

Brickmakers Arms

RAILWAY LINE

STATION

RAILWAY VIEW HOTEL

BRICKPITS

All these shops are empty

This is the laundry where Mum and Auntie Adie work.

Archie lives here. He's a bully. He picks on me if I walk down this street!

BRICKPITS

The kid here got gastro

BRICKPITS

There's some houses here they never finished

Iceworks

POSH SCHOOL

BIG TREE

POSH KIDS KEEP THEIR CRICKET AND FOOTBALL STUFF HERE

There's a farm I forgot

Müllers workshop.

My mate Tom Müller lives here with his mum and dad and Freddie and their Auntie

My PLACE!

LANE

The cows for the dairy live here

Ned Kelly grazes here

MORE BRICKPITS

My dad used to work here but he got a bad cough and the boss told him to leave.

CREEK TRACK

CREEK TRACK

CANAL - Dad built this

They're building a new factory here. Maybe my dad can get a job here.

Some sort of ironworks

Vegetable garden

new road

All weeds and rubbish

Bridge

All this is weeds, but sometimes pumpkin comes up all by itself. Yuk, I hate pumpkin.

Once a month, Mr Merry has a party. It's called the Labor Party, and it's just grown-ups sitting in his room and talking. Miss Müller goes, but Mum and Auntie Adie don't. Mr Merry gives Tom and me a shilling to nick up to the pub and bring them back some beer. He lets us keep the change!

This is me and Ned Kelly. He's the front horse on Mr Müller's bus. Mr Müller reckons you've got to be an outlaw, to beat the new trams. I'd like to be a tram driver when I grow up, but most people round here make bricks, so maybe I will too. Mr Merry reckons every brick in every house tells a story.

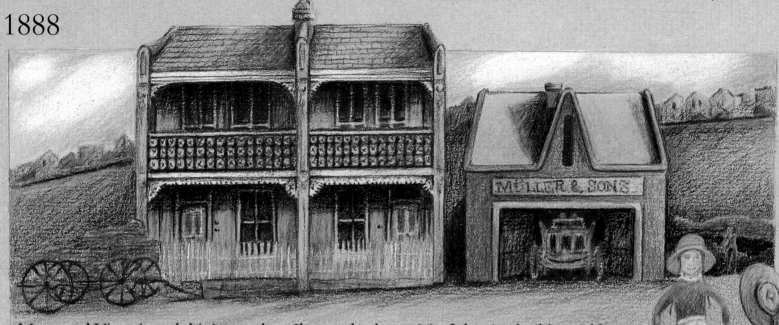

My name's Victoria and this is my place. I'm nearly eleven. My father is a builder and he built our house, and Father and Mother and Wesley and Charles and May and I are the first people ever to live here! Father built the next door house too, for the Müllers, and now he's started two more houses on the other side. Our house is the biggest. We've got three bedrooms upstairs, and downstairs there's a parlour and a dining-room, then the breezeway, then the kitchen. We've even got tap water. Mother says it's like a Dream Come True, but sometimes Father looks worried.

This is a map of my place. Mother reckons you get sick if you even look at the creek, but Father says it'll get better soon when they finish making the sewerage. Sometimes I play on the swing in the big tree, but the Owen girls don't talk to me. As if I'd care! The hotel's just changed its name because of the Centenary. Mother won't even let me walk on that side of the road. We're all in the Temperance League.

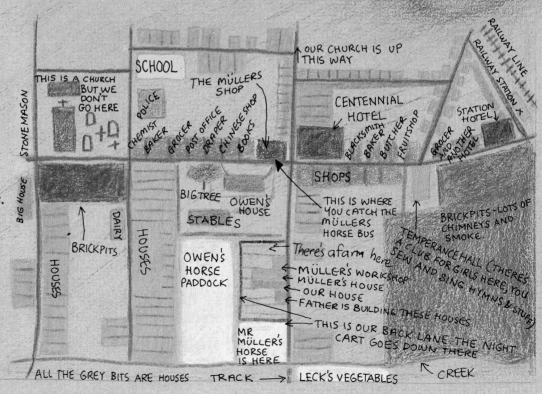

THIS IS A CHURCH BUT WE DON'T GO HERE

SCHOOL

OUR CHURCH IS UP THIS WAY

THE MÜLLERS SHOP

STONE MASON

POLICE

CHEMIST

BAKER

GROCER

POST OFFICE

DRAPER

CHINESE SHOP

BOOKS

CENTENNIAL HOTEL

BLACKSMITH

BAKER

BUTCHER

FRUITSHOP

STATION HOTEL

GROCER AND ANOTHER HOTEL

RAILWAY LINE

RAILWAY STATION X

BIG HOUSE

BIG TREE

OWEN'S HOUSE

STABLES

SHOPS

THIS IS WHERE YOU CATCH THE MÜLLERS HORSE BUS

BRICKPITS - LOTS OF CHIMNEYS AND SMOKE.

BRICKPITS

DAIRY

HOUSES

HOUSES

OWEN'S HORSE PADDOCK

There's a farm here

MÜLLER'S WORKSHOP

MÜLLER'S HOUSE

OUR HOUSE

FATHER IS BUILDING THESE HOUSES

TEMPERANCE HALL (THERE'S A CLUB FOR GIRLS HERE, YOU SEW AND SING HYMNS & STUFF)

MR MÜLLER'S HORSE IS HERE

THIS IS OUR BACK LANE. THE NIGHT CART GOES DOWN THERE

ALL THE GREY BITS ARE HOUSES   TRACK →   LECK'S VEGETABLES   ← CREEK

This year, Australia had its hundredth birthday! We went to the Centennial Picnic in our neighbours' horse bus. Miss Müller says that the country is really as old as Time, and that other people were living here, long before all of us. Father says that's the kind of idea that you'd expect from a woman who goes to work in the city. (Mother is always telling me that ladies don't have jobs, but I want to be something when I grow up. Miss Müller even catches the morning train, with all the men.)

This is me and Squarker. Sometimes he gives you a real fright. Once he made the dunny can man drop everything.

1878

This is my place. My name's really Heinrich, but everyone except my grandparents calls me Henry. I'm ten. When my mother died, Minna stopped being a teacher, and she looks after Father and Anna and me. I used to have a little brother too, but he got the gastro. My grandparents and Uncle Wolf live on top of the new shop. My grandfather says that one day I will own it, but I want to be a balloonist. I didn't tell him that.

MÜLLER & SONS

This is me and Gretchen. She's Minna's cat, but she's mine too.

Stone mason

I go to school here

Church

wheelwright
the new post office
draper
grocer
bootmaker

houses

Our new shop where we sell Saddlery. My grandparents live upstairs.

Bay View Hotel

blacksmith
baker
butcher
grocer

There are gas lights all along the road now.

Brickmaker's Arms

big house

BRICKYARD

Big tree

Roses

The Owens live here

Mr Owen has sold this. There's going to be shops.

The carter's yard

brickpits

Chimneys

DAIRY

More cows

Stables

a little farm

The people here look after the cows

This is a map of my place. I get over the fence and climb the big tree and pretend I'm on a balloon. The creek's so dirty, Minna won't let me play in it. She says it's like an open sewer, and that's why my brother Siggie died.

They're starting to build houses here

Big work-shop where we make saddles and harnesses.

Mr Owen's horses

Our house

my grandfather has bought our land from Mr Owen.

well

Cows—but my father says this will be Sold soon.

This is the Creek. It smells.

stepping stones
this is where I saw the dragon

This is where our vegetables come from.

Bridge

One night I woke up and there was all this banging and yelling.
I crept out into the street and it was coming from Mr Wong's garden.
So I went across the stepping stones, and there was a dragon!

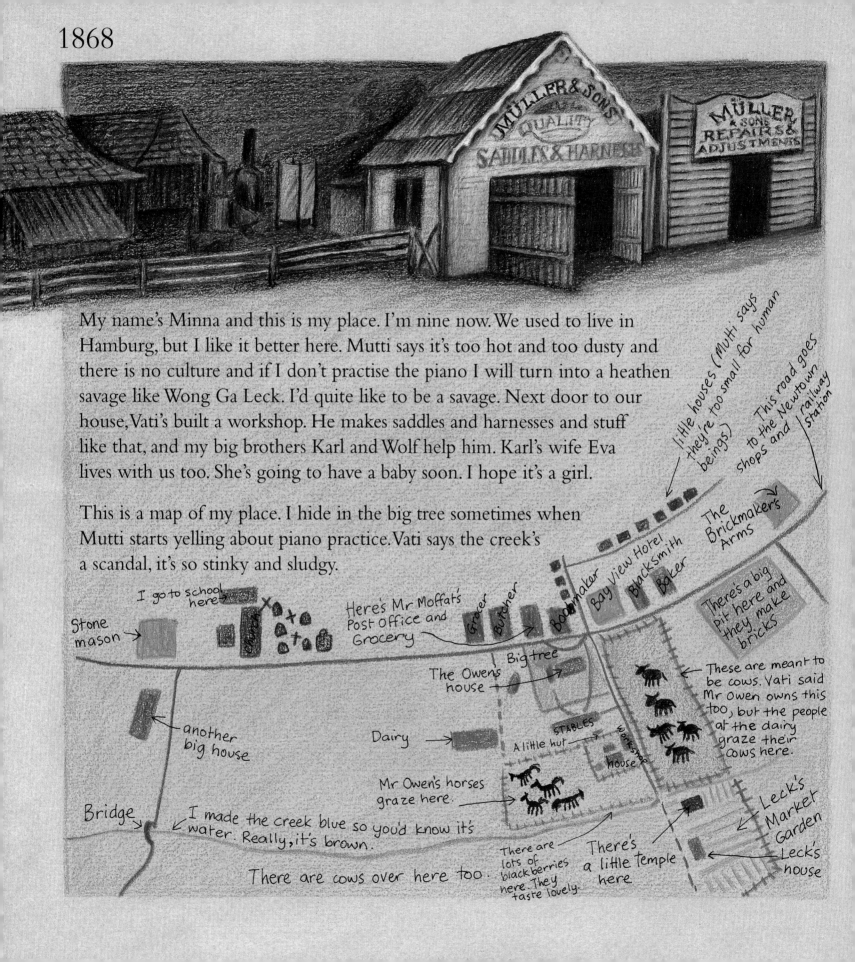

My name's Minna and this is my place. I'm nine now. We used to live in Hamburg, but I like it better here. Mutti says it's too hot and too dusty and there is no culture and if I don't practise the piano I will turn into a heathen savage like Wong Ga Leck. I'd quite like to be a savage. Next door to our house, Vati's built a workshop. He makes saddles and harnesses and stuff like that, and my big brothers Karl and Wolf help him. Karl's wife Eva lives with us too. She's going to have a baby soon. I hope it's a girl.

This is a map of my place. I hide in the big tree sometimes when Mutti starts yelling about piano practice. Vati says the creek's a scandal, it's so stinky and sludgy.

little houses (Mutti says they're too small for human beings)

This road goes to the Newtown shops and railway station

The Brickmaker's Arms

Bootmaker
Bay View Hotel
Blacksmith
Baker

There's a big pit here and they make bricks

I go to school here

Stone mason

Church

Here's Mr Moffat's Post Office and Grocery

Grocer
Butcher

Big tree

The Owen's house

These are meant to be cows. Vati said Mr Owen owns this too, but the people at the dairy graze their cows here.

another big house

Dairy

STABLES
A little hut
Workshop
house

Mr Owen's horses graze here.

Bridge

I made the creek blue so you'd know it's water. Really, it's brown.

There are cows over here too.

There are lots of blackberries here. They taste lovely.

There's a little Temple here

Leck's Market Garden
Leck's house

At Christmas time, we have a proper German party, with a fir tree and candles. Then we sing around the piano. It still seems funny, without any snow. But the food tastes just as good.

This is me and my kitten Gretchen. Leck gave her to me. Some of the other kids chase after Leck and pull his pigtail, but he's my friend.

1858

This is my place. My name's Benjamin Franklin and I am twelve years old. I was born in San Francisco but Mother says Dad got Gold Fever. First we went to the Californian fields, but he didn't find anything, so we moved to Australia and he tried his luck out Bathurst way. And when that was no good, we moved here. Now Dad works for Mr Moffatt, but I don't think he likes it.

Last Thanksgiving, Mother cooked a turkey like she used to do at home. Sometimes I wish I wasn't American, because the other kids laugh at how I speak, but Dad says one day everyone in the world will be free and equal and like brothers and sisters. When I think how Beth and Amy and I fight, I don't reckon it'll be much different.

This is Tripod. I share her with Leck. We found her one day down the back of the joss house. The other kids tease Leckie too, so we stick together.

This is a map of my place. The creek's too dirty to swim in, but Leck and I make boats and race them down it. Sometimes we hide up in the big tree and throw the figs down at the kids who call us things.

Inn

Druggist Butcher's shop Mr Moffat's grocery. Dad works here.

→ Houses

I go to school here + Leckie doesn't.

Minister's house

church

cemetery

farrier

BAY VIEW HOTEL

There's a railway station up at Newtown now. It takes about twenty minutes to walk there if you go really fast.

Dr Cheadle's house

There's a big

hole here

big tree

Posh House. The Owens live here It's like a castle!!

Stables and coach yard

My Place Dad rents it from the Owens

Bridge

The Creek (Amy fell in and Leckie got her out)

Some old orange trees

Joss House (Leckie's church)

Swampy land – lots of birds and tadpoles.

down this way there's the river

Stepping Stones

Leck's house →

Market garden

There's factories and stuff over here ↓

track →

My name's Johanna and this is my place. Soon I'll be ten. I live here with Granny Sarah because my ma died when she had me. She was called Alice. Granny Sarah grows vegetables, and I help her carry them around to people's houses and sell them. We use creek water for the garden, but you can't drink it. There's a woolwashery up near the swamp and they drain all their yuk into our creek!

This is a map of my place. Sometimes I creep into the Owens' garden and climb the big tree. If Mr Owen catches me, he gives me a weird look, but he just stomps away. Granny Sarah says I'm never to go there.

Granny Sarah says the river's got really dirty here since they built the dam.

This house is really big but only three people live there

There's a school at the church now (I'm glad I don't have to go.)

new houses (we sell vegetables to the people)

My mother and grandfather are buried here

dam

Inn

another Inn

Brady's Inn

houses

we sell vegetables to the people down here. (It's a mile to walk)

church and cemetery

Mr Owen's tannery and woollen mills down this way. Poo. They stink.

• = big tree
■ = Owen's place
✗ = My Place
✕ = the Bay View Hotel
▨ = Mr Owen's land
🏠 = Big houses
▬ = Shops. There's five!

Last time Uncle Sam came home, we had a party. He's a sailor and you'd never guess what he brought me! Auntie Maryann got a half-holiday. She's Mrs Owen's upstairs maid. Uncle Davey still lived here then, but he's gone out Bathurst way now to be a shepherd for Mr Charles, and Granny Sarah says that one day we might move there too. She reckons too many people live here now, and she's fed up to the teeth with the dust of the main road and all the traffic.

This is me and Mischief. Isn't he beautiful!

This is my place. I'm Davey, and I'm seven. Just Ma and me live here now, because Alice and Maryann live up at the new house and are maids. Sam's my brother, but he's on a ship catching whales. He's fourteen.

Before Sam went away, Mr Owen was shot by bushrangers, so Mr John became the master. Ma says he's even worse. Mr John's sold most of the farm, and there are three more big houses now between here and the river.

This is a map of my place. When the wind blows the wrong way, it stinks from Mr John's tannery. Ma says we're really lucky we're up the good end of the creek, but she won't eat the oysters any more. There's a swing in the big tree for Mr John's kids and I'm not allowed to play on it. So I climb up and drop figs on them, and they run away. Once Mr John caught me and whipped me, but it was worth it. They're snobs.

lime kilns

There is a new dam here with a bridge across the top

Inn

← Mr Owen was shot up this way.

Road - lots of people drive along he from Sydney to go for picnics b the river

BIG house

little houses (fishermen and lime workers)

WATER

CREEK

The Owen's tannery and woollen mill are down this way

When I was little, my father fell off the roof of the new house and died. Ma says she hates the Owens and all their works. I don't really remember him, but one night last summer Ma took me to the creek and lit a big campfire. We stayed up all night, and she told me how Dad discovered the swimming hole!

This is the new church. My dad is buried here.

There's a horse trough here now

Brady's Inn

To New Town then to Sydney

Little farms and houses

This is all swampy land (no fish but lots of frogs!)

you can cross the creek here

✗ = My Place
✝ = Church is being built here
● = big tree
● = New House (Owens)
▪ = Mr John Owen has kept this land
▪ = Mr Owen used to own all this and more, but after he died Mr John divided it up and sold it.
● = This is the swimming hole my dad found.

This is me and Duchess. She belongs to Mr John, but the groom lets me brush her. Next year I'm starting work as a stable boy.

1828

My name's Alice and this is my place. I'm nine and a quarter. Another girl called Alice lived here once, but she died, and Ma gave me her name. The Owens used to live here, but they're staying in Sydney Town till their new house is built. Mr John still often comes back to check on things. Ma and Dad live here too of course, and Maryann and Little Sam. Dad's in charge of the farm and the convicts. They're making a quarry to get stone for the new house. I take them their lunch.

This is me and Wilhemina.
She loves it when I scratch her back.

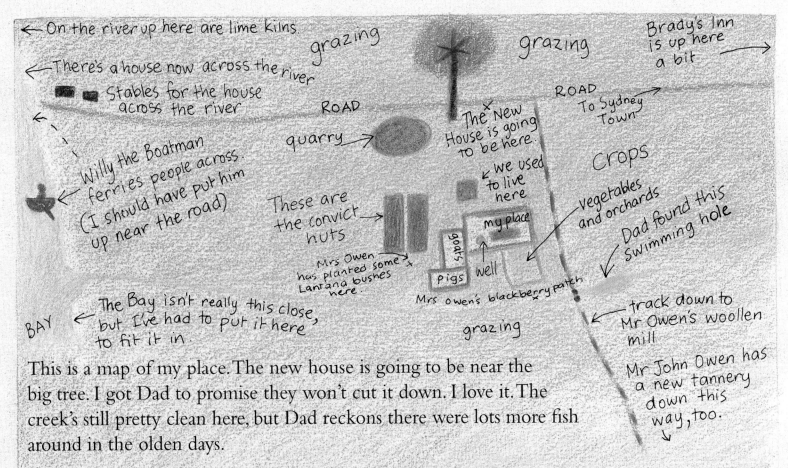

On the river up here are lime kilns. ←

grazing

grazing

Brady's Inn is up here a bit →

There's a house now across the river ←

Stables for the house across the river

ROAD

To Sydney Town

ROAD

The New House is going to be here.

quarry →

Crops

Willy the Boatman ferries people across. (I should have put him up near the road) ←

we used to live here →

These are the convict huts →

my place

Vegetables and orchards

Dad found this swimming hole →

Mrs Owen has planted some Lantana bushes here.

goats

pigs   well

Mrs Owen's blackberry patch

BAY ← The Bay isn't really this close, but I've had to put it here, to fit it in

grazing

← track down to Mr Owen's woollen mill

Mr John Owen has a new tannery down this way, too.

This is a map of my place. The new house is going to be near the big tree. I got Dad to promise they won't cut it down. I love it. The creek's still pretty clean here, but Dad reckons there were lots more fish around in the olden days.

The night the Owens went, we all had a party. Dad used to be a convict too, so he doesn't treat the men like slaves, like Mr Owen and Mr John do. Ma roasted a whole sheep, and Old Freddie danced on the table.

This is my place. My name's Charles and I'm eight and a half. I live here with my mother and my brother John and my sister Meg, and sometimes my father. I had another sister called Alice but she died. Sam and Sarah are our servants. Sam is in charge of things because Father is mostly in Sydney. John says Father is making money. He's got a new woollen mill across the swamp. John says he's going to make money too when he grows up, but I want to be a farmer.

This is me and Daisy.
Sarah taught me to milk her.
Sarah's nice. She lets me turn
the handle on the butter-churn,
and drink the buttermilk.

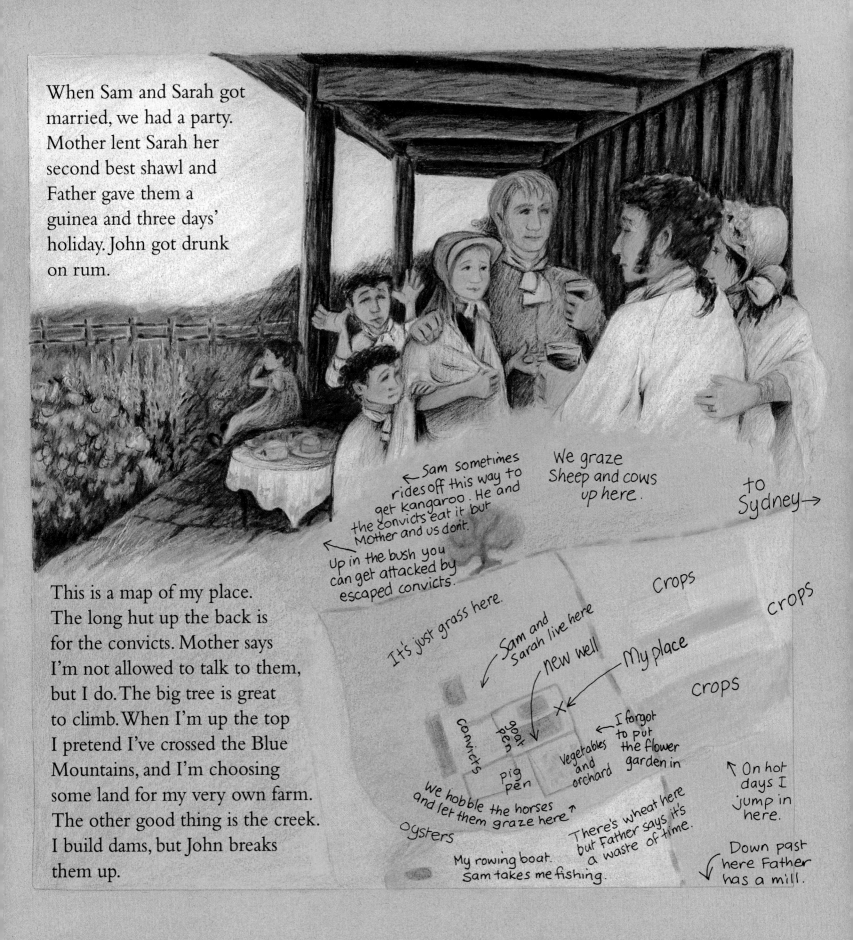

When Sam and Sarah got married, we had a party. Mother lent Sarah her second best shawl and Father gave them a guinea and three days' holiday. John got drunk on rum.

This is a map of my place. The long hut up the back is for the convicts. Mother says I'm not allowed to talk to them, but I do. The big tree is great to climb. When I'm up the top I pretend I've crossed the Blue Mountains, and I'm choosing some land for my very own farm. The other good thing is the creek. I build dams, but John breaks them up.

My name's Sarah and this is my place. I'm nine. I was born in Sydney but my mother came from England on a convict ship. Last year she died so Mrs Owen took me as a servant. She doesn't beat me much, but you should see all the work I have to do! Mrs Owen lives here too of course, and Alice and the baby John. Mr Owen's mainly in Sydney, doing business. Mrs Owen runs the farm, and she has five convict servants and Sam to help her. Sam used to be a convict but now he's a ticket-of-leave man. He's more like my family than anyone else in the world.

This is me and Pokey. I call her that because she pokes her head into my lean-to at night. I steal crusts for her, and she's learning to eat from my hand. She's my secret.

One day, some soldiers came to see Mr Owen. They ate and drank a lot, and talked about kicking out Governor Bligh. I hate it when adults get drunk and talk politics, so I nicked some jam roly and some oranges, and Alice and I went up to the big tree and had our own party.

Mr Owen owns the land across here too. The whole farm is 650 acres (Mrs Owen says) He uses this for grazing.

TO SYDNEY TOWN

Other people have farms further up the track but you don't see them much.

← At the end of the track, there's the river. There's a kind of ford.
← to river

The Big Tree

Mr Owen's horse

I can't draw the → crops. But Sam says there are 23 acres wheat 20 acres maize 4 acres barley & oats ½ acre peas, beans, spuds

This is a map of my place. I look after the vegetables, and they taste great. The wheat and stuff all goes to Sydney. Sam swims in a deep hole in the creek but I'm not allowed to.

Sam's hut
kitchen
chimney
cottage
convict's hut
VEGETABLE GARDEN & ORCHARD
where I sleep

we cross the creek on stepping stones

Sam's swimming hole

I get oysters down the end of the creek. Sam goes fishing in the bay. He catches lots.

goat pen (11 goats)
pig pen (18 pigs)
Mrs Owen has planted a blackberry garden here X
I have to water them.

Walking track

This is my place. My name's Sam, and I was born in London. I'm eleven. The judge put me in gaol because I stole a jacket. I was cold. In the gaol they beat me. Then they put me on a ship and sent me here. Then they let me out to work for Mr Owen. Sometimes he whips me too. But at least it's not cold, and I can catch heaps of fish to eat.

Last Christmas, Mr Owen gave me a holiday. Mrs Owen is still in England and she sent out a pudding. Mr Owen drank a lot of rum and let me eat as much as I liked. I've never had a pudding or a holiday before.

This is me and Katie. I milk her every morning, and at night I put her in the pen in case she wanders away.

Mr Owen sometimes goes this way to shoot a kangaroo

I sit here

Further up this way → some freed convicts have little farms.

Mr Owen walks this way to Sydney Cove. The track runs along the ridge.

Mr Owen's hut

I nearly trod on a snake here.

Katie's Pen

I sleep here →

We've cleared all this (chopping down trees and burning). We're planting corn.

Swampy land

Orange trees

There are stepping stones here

This is my swimming hole. I found it!

Mr Owen owns all this too but we haven't cleared it yet.

The creek goes into the river, then Botany Bay. If I had a good boat I could sail right back to London. (If I knew the way)

This is a map of my place. We're clearing the bush back to make a farm. It gives me blisters. Mr Owen has 90 acres, but he wants to buy more. I think he's got too much already. Sometimes he goes off to Sydney Cove to get supplies, and doesn't come back for a week. I get scared at night then, but in the daytime I nick down to the creek. I've found a great swimming hole.

At the top of the hill there's a big tree. I climb up it and pretend I can see all the way to Shoreditch. That's where my mother is, and my sisters and brother. I wish I had someone to play with.

My name's Barangaroo. I belong to this place. We're staying here for the summer, at the creek camp, to get the fish down in the bay. But often we stay a while at other places. Everywhere we go is home. I live with my parents and my brother Bereewan and my grandparents and my aunties and uncles and cousins. We take our tools and our hunting and fishing stuff with us when we move, but of course we leave the huts and canoes here for next time. Sometimes I wonder what it would be like to stop in the same place always, but my grandmother says no one does that. I guess it would be boring.

This is a map of this place. We camp here because the creek water's so fresh and good, and we're close to the river and the bay. In the creek there's a great swimming hole where my cousins and I always play. My father says he swam in exactly the same place when he was a boy, and my grandfather says he did too. At the top of the hill there's a big fig tree.

THE RIVER

we fish up the river too

My father and the other men go up this way to get kangaroo.

big tree on hill

the huts

there are big stepping stones here

Mangrove trees

The fires keep the mossies away.

The Bay

mud flats good oysters

good crabs

The creek

Swampy land

there's heaps of fish

We keep the canoes here.
We all go out fishing in the bay.

Swimming hole

This is our dog. He sleeps with me.

Last week a whale got washed up on the bay, so we invited some other people from round about, and had a big barbecue. As well as the meat, we had piles of vegetables, and oysters and pippies and crabs and octopus and I've forgotten what else. I ate so much I thought I'd explode. Then I fell asleep till the night-time party started.